COFFEE, TEA, OR ME?

TL TRAVIS

Sapphire Publishing

COFFEE, TEA, OR ME?

Trademark Acknowledgement – Coffee, Tea, or Me

The author acknowledges the trademark status and trademark owners of the following wordmarks mentioned in this work of fiction:

Lady and the Tramp: Disney Enterprises

Ben & Jerry: Ben & Jerry's Homemade, Inc.

Star Wars: Lucasfilm Ltd; Disney Enterprises

Indiana Jones: Paramount Pictures; Lucasfilm; Walt Disney Pictures

Grindr: Nearby Buddy Finder, LLC

Food Network: Television Food Network, G.P.

Kindle: Amazon Technologies

Netflix: Netflix, Inc.

Contents

CHAPTER ONE

Howie

Every day as the ten a.m. rush barrels in, he graces us with his presence, and by us I mean me. His usual morning order for which he never falters from is a medium soy no foam latte, at kid's temp with a butterscotch scone under the name of Jackson. In the afternoon, he switches to iced tea and a BLT on sourdough. I smile, unabashedly bat my eyelashes and watch him walk away, ignoring my advances and acting as though I don't exist. Like straight up, no eye contact, could give two shits less blatantly ignores me. *Story of my life.*

I scan his credit card, and hand it back as he mutters a menial thanks before taking his usual spot at the corner table next to the outlet bar. He erects his mobile office, plugs in his laptop, inserts his ear buds and buries his nose in his next big release while waiting for us to deliver his goods. *Why do I always want the men who don't want me?*

Outwardly, I sigh and wait on the next customer in line and Lexi prepares their requests as my dream man walks away. I watch her deliver his order; without glancing up he mumbles another half-assed thank you, his focus never wavering. Seems whatever is on the screen is far more important than we, the humans he's paid to do his bidding, are. Lexi eyes me and shrugs, returning to her duties. For literal months this has been going on. *What gives?*

I seem to be one of the few millennials who enjoy interacting with other humans, I crave it really. The cold, lifeless feel of an electronic device versus a warm smile has no appeal to me whatsoever. My friends are forever buried nose deep in their phones when we go out, at times the frustration mounts until I reach my breaking point, snatching it from their clutches in order to gain their attention. Apologies generally follow, but they seem forced as opposed to heartfelt.

More and more I find myself alone, stuffing my face full of frozen goodness, thanking my friends Ben & Jerry for keeping me company as my so-called acquaintances hit the club scene without me. Why they go as a group I'll never know because as soon as they have their drinks in hand, they're off scanning the room for hookups which has never been my cup of tea. Sure, I can't deny I've had my fair share, but each one left me feeling used which took me days afterward to shake. I need a living, breathing connection. One with feelings, hopes and dreams. Someone who will want to stay around long after the sexual portion of the evening is over. Someone with similar interests as I who likes visiting museums, shares in my love of zoos and aquariums. Far too often, it seems once or twice with me is all they can handle before moving on.

Am I truly that repulsive?

Is dreaming of the fairy-tale life, white picket fence, two point five kids and a dog no longer anyone's desire? Am I destined to die alone, or should I conform and accept that all I'm going to get out of life is a series of random, nameless hook-ups? Is that all that I'm worth? Guys tell me what I want to hear when we first meet, then once they get in my pants they're gone as quickly as they came. Literally, bust a nut and out the door they run. I tried to cuddle with one guy afterward; he took off out the door with his pants and shoes in hand. I showered, changed the sheets, and curled up in the fetal position and cried myself to sleep.

Night after night I roll over, longing to find a warm body beside me to snuggle with. Stick my cold feet against their skin and giggle as they whisper half assed threats while smiling lovingly back at me. He'd roll over, tickling me until I'm left breathless then hold me as I nod off in his arms.

"Let it go honey." Lexi touches my forearm, drawing me from my pity party for one. Something she's had to do far too often as of late. "I don't think it's you, he ignores everyone." She always knows what I'm thinking, some self-deprecating thought as to why I'm unworthy of being loved.

"Sometimes he orders coffee, sometimes he orders tea. Oh, how I wished one time he'd order me," I mumbled aloud, immediately wishing I could take the words back.

"Working on your poetry I see," Lexi teased as she headed into the backroom.

I suppose these feelings of worthlessness stem from being raised in the foster care system, bouncing from family to family as new kids came in. Some families only wanted to have you until a certain age, some only cared about you for the monthly stipend they'd receive. Some, well they weren't worthy of the gum stuck to the bottom of my worn-out sneakers. Once I graduated high school and turned eighteen, I was cut loose, forced to couch surf from friend to friend, finally landing on Lexi's sofa and in this job. She and her mom own this coffee shop we both work at and lived in the apartment above it. They were, well still are, great to me. I stayed with them until I saved enough money to get a place of my own. They were the first humans to ever treat me like family.

Lexi lives with her boyfriend James in the apartment above the store now. Her mom retired last year and moved to sunny Florida. She's living the life in her fifty plus community and seems to be the life of the party there from the stories she shares. It was always a dream of hers and the timing worked out perfectly. With Lexi assuming the role of owner-operator, she immediately promoted me to the assistant manager position and with the pay increase, I was able to obtain a studio apartment within walking distance of the cafe. Not something that's easily obtained by Seattle standards.

Last summer, James presented Lexi and her mom Ann with a proposal to add a bookstore to the coffee shop. There was a large area we used a small portion of for storage, the rest was wasted space. That was the area he recommended be a large part of the remodel along with a small section of the dining area with a pass through connecting both spaces. He reiterated the fact that readers needed coffee and a place to sit and enjoy their new book purchases.

Once they crunched the numbers, they found the rental income to be gained from his proposed book shop made his offer far too lucrative to pass up. After meeting with the bank, it was agreed upon and the remodel took place. Six months ago, we re-launched our new brand *Caffeinated Books and More* and business has been booming since.

The neighborhood reception was overwhelming, and James had just the right amount of space to house his inventory and even added a local author section. Of course, if one wanted to do a signing it would need to be held on the café side as there was only enough room in his space for his counter and bookshelves. That's where Jackson entered the picture.

The memory is so vivid it's as though it happened only yesterday...

The bell above the door chimed. I was leaning over with my back to it, wiping the tables clean. When I turned, our eyes locked. I felt the heat as it surged through me; I know I didn't make that up but just as quickly as it came it was washed away like the Seattle rain.

"Welcome to Caffeinated Books, how can we help you?" James' deep voice drew attention to the fact we weren't alone. When the handsome man staring back at me didn't say anything in return, James cleared his throat.

Reluctantly, his gaze left mine, a wave of emptiness surged through me. "Um, yes, hello. My name is Jackson Milsap. I'm a writer and was wondering if you offered local authors' literary works for sale here?"

Awkwardly I stared, burning every nuance, every inflection of that man's voice, all things associated with Jackson Milsap into the vault in my brain.

"Excuse me!" an unfamiliar, demanding voice called startling me from reliving my treasured flashback as the body associated with it rudely tapped its knuckles against the counter. "Hellooo? Are you working or not?"

I heard the hinges of the swinging doors that led to the back protest as Lexi pushed her way through them.

"Yes, sorry. How can I help you?" I asked, even though my gut instinct was to kick this jackass to the curb. There was no way killing him with kindness was going to pay off.

"It's about time. I've been standing here for ten minutes trying to get your attention," he continued berating me even though I'd already apologized.

"I'm sorry, what can I get for you?" I tried again, catching sight of Jackson watching this uncomfortable interaction exacerbated my flustered state. More than anything, I wanted this guy to leave before his sharp words reduced me to tears which I knew was only moments away.

"I'd like to speak to a manager. I mean really," he demanded, staring at his watch while angrily shaking his head.

"I— I am the manager," I stuttered, losing sight of the situation at hand as I felt a lifetime of repressed feelings from being bullied and told I was worthless rush to the surface.

"Well, if that's the case then I'm sure this place won't be open for long," the pompous ass snickered.

"Howie?" Lexi tapped my shoulder. I'd never even heard her walk up beside me. "Can you get me another bottle of vanilla syrup please? I'll watch the front." I knew she didn't need it since she'd restocked after the morning rush. This was her way of removing me from the situation at hand. She always knew what I needed before I did, which was one of many reasons why I loved my bestie. Without a second look, I darted from the scene, scrambling into the office in the back room and sunk to the floor, releasing the waterworks.

CHAPTER TWO

Jackson

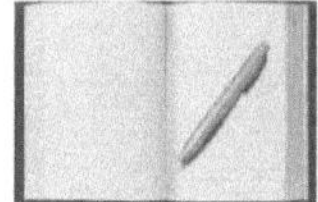

I don't know what came over me but watching that man disrespect Howie the way he had sent me over an edge I'd never crossed. Not being one for confrontation, I surprised myself as my feet swiftly carried me mere inches from where he stood, and my mouth formed the words that my brain didn't know it had cocked and loaded.

"What gives you the right to treat someone that way? Didn't your mother teach you any manners?" The fire raging inside me as I towered over this man was like none I'd ever felt before. Never had I spoken more than my order aloud either for books or coffee in here until this very moment. Always I sat quietly, sneaking glances of the man I desired as he worked. How dare this imbecile treat such a kind soul so horrifically.

"Wha— what?" he stammered, taking a step back.

"You heard me. Do you work in customer service?" I asked. Vehemently he shook his head no. "How would you feel if someone came into your place of business and treated you with the amount of disrespect you just showed him?"

He squared his shoulders, attempting to fluff himself up far more than was possible, "I wouldn't like it. But I waited ten..." He trailed off as I held my hand up to stop him.

"Don't even go there. From the time you walked in until the time you started knocking on the counter like you didn't have an ounce of class was less than two minutes."

"Well, I've never been treated so poorly. I have a good mind to leave and never come back here," he huffed.

"There's the door," Lexi told him, pointing toward the entrance. "Have a great day." As he stormed past the line of customers, they clapped, and one even whistled.

"Howie?" I questioned her.

"Go ahead back, he's probably in the office."

It was now or never. I'd already set the wheels in motion by sticking up for him, so it was high time I grew a pair and finally asked the man who'd held my attention longer than any other out on a real date.

Crossing through the swinging door, my heart pounded, echoing loudly in my ears. Anxiety coursed through me forcing me to stop and take several deep breaths to tamper it. While I stood there centering myself, I scanned the storage area, spotting a small room to the left and leaned around the door to peek inside. I could hear Howie's sobs as I knocked on the half open door. When I saw him, the need to scoop him up and cradle him in my arms surprised me as I eyed his small frame curled up on the floor.

"Is he gone?" he asked, when he glanced up at the shocked look crossing his delicate features clearly said I wasn't who he was expecting to see.

"Yes, are you okay?" I pulled a couple of tissues from the box atop the filing cabinet, handing them to him.

"I'm so embarrassed," he complained, dabbing at his eyes and blowing his nose.

"Don't be, he's gone and he's not worth the emotion." I crouched beside him.

"That was awesome!" Lexi sang as she entered the already overcrowded space.

"That was so not awesome," Howie defensively argued.

"You missed it, Jackson put him in his place. He rambled stupid shit about us not staying in business for long and I told him where the door was. The other patrons cheered as he left." She spun in the desk chair, laughing as I felt the heated flush snake up my neck.

"You, you stuck up for me?" His hazel eyes stared expectantly back at me. All I wanted to do was take his pain away but could only manage a nod as the English language seemed to have escaped me.

"I'll just, um…" Lexi said, heading out the door and closing it behind her.

"No one but Lexi has ever stood up for me before. Thank you," he said, barely above a whisper.

His words saddened me. Had no one ever really done that? How could anyone discount this beautiful man's feelings?

"You're welcome." I stood, extending a hand to help him up. "Um, Howie. Would you— Do you— Ugh, I'm majorly screwing this up." Flustered, I ran my hands through my hair. More than likely standing it on end and looking like I'd sprouted horns. When he giggled, I opened my eyes, losing myself in his captivating smile and summoned the nerve to begin again. "Are you seeing anyone?"

"Nope," he replied, accentuating the '*p*' with a pop before drawing his bottom lip between his teeth. My eyes followed the action, filling me with the need to remove it with my own two lips.

"Wouldyouliketogooutwithme?" There, I said it. It may've come out like one long fucking-word, but at least the words I'd been working up the courage to say for months were finally free. It felt like a weight had been lifted, and I released the breath I'd held while speaking.

"I think I caught the gist of that," he teased. "Either you're asking me to go outside with you, or you're asking me out on a date?" His sly grin said he knew what the right answer was, but he was enjoying the change of tides as I was now the one left suffering.

"Um, the second one?" Even I'd become unsure at this point.

"I thought you'd never ask." Standing on his tiptoes, he kissed my cheek.

Once again, I blushed. "Yeah, seems the writer has trouble finding his words. That probably isn't good for business." Outwardly, I tried my best to remain calm but on the inside I was dancing. Being an introvert had its positives and negatives. Writing was the perfect career for those of us who were socially challenged, but with every passing day my desire for Howie increased at an alarming rate and I knew I needed to crack the shell I'd erected around myself in order to do something about it. I just hadn't expected it to come out in the form of a confrontation.

"I need to get back out front. Can I get your number so we can text the deets for our date?" he asked. I handed him my phone and he keyed in his number, shooting himself a text causing the *Star Wars* cantina song to sound from his pocket.

"Nice ringtone." Being a *Star Wars* fan myself, this was a positive first sign in my book.

"I flip back and forth between that one and the *Indiana Jones* theme song. Thank you again, Jackson" he said, sincerely. "What you did meant more to me than you'll ever know."

CHAPTER THREE

Howie

Did that really just happen? Pinch me, I may be dreaming.

I returned to the front totally dazed, forgetting he was behind me until the palm of his hand grazed the small of my back. Shivers coursed through as the man I'd been pining after for months slid by me in the narrow area. I don't know whose actions I was more surprised by. Jackson's— for not only reciting more than his order to me and for him turning out to be some sort of knight in shining espresso. Or at myself— for the brazen act of kissing his cheek. Given the fact that I'd wanted to tackle him to the ground and cover every inch of his body with my lips, I'd have to say the kiss was probably the wiser path for me to have chosen.

"You all right, doll?" Lexi whispered to me, tracking my line of sight to Jackson's table.

"He, he asked me out." I turned my surprised gaze on her.

"Yes!" she loudly cheered, fist bumping the air as all eyes turned our way, including his.

"Shh, keep your voice down." I glanced toward his table, hoping for the first time his attention was on his screen and not on us, but his pale blue eyes were glued to me.

"Where? When? You must tell me now!" she begged, using her best mad scientist voice. Before I could respond, my phone vibrated inside my pocket.

"Ugh…" I groaned.

"What?" Lexi questioned, trying to see the screen.

"He heard you." I put my hands over my face in a feeble attempt at hiding.

"How do you know?" she asked, so I showed her the text.

Tell her I'll pick you up at seven Saturday night.

Her laughter rang out through the small café as I sunk to the ground behind the counter. Today was only Wednesday, how was I going to make it through the next four days?

Jackson and I texted several times during the remainder of the week, and I was surprised to see the dialogue between us In the end, we decided on dinner, as you did on most first dates, and from there we'd see how the evening progressed. I was guessing... having never really dated before, so more likely I was assuming dinner was first date etiquette. *Maybe I've watched one too many rom coms.* Ugh, this had imminent failure written all over it as I had no freaking idea what in the hell I was doing and to top it off I'd offered to cook at my place. *Great, twenty-two-years old and going on my first date. How fucking sad was that?*

CHAPTER FOUR

Jackson

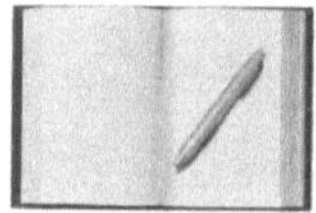

What was I doing?

What should I wear?

What if I'm too boring for him?

This was exactly why I never dated, merely resorted to nameless Grindr hook-ups to avoid the formalities of getting to know someone. I'd been told multiple times over the years I had the personality of a zit which only further drove me into myself. Hopefully, I could manage to be human enough for Howie.

Trevor Marshall was my first love. We met my sopho-more year at college. He was everything to me, but after six months of dating he decided I was too boring, and he moved on. Taking my heart with him. After that, I reverted back to my former self, shutting the world out and creating new ones of my own. Now, eight years later and on the verge of turning thirty, I've allowed the barriers to come down and it scared the ever-loving shit out of me. It took me years to get past the pain of losing my first love which was only compounded as I'd see him and his new flavor of the week strolling hand in hand through the courtyard. He went through men like underwear but always paraded them around like awards. The only saving grace was that he was a senior while I was still a junior, so the visual misery was short lived. *Out of sight doesn't always mean out of mind.*

The time for grieving has long since passed, son. Put on your big boy pants and allow another in, my mother would say if that beautiful woman was still here with me today.

I'd forgotten to not only ask what kind of wine he pre-ferred after we decided to move our date to his place for dinner, but what he was making so I could properly pair the two. This omission left me selecting one of each to err on the side of caution.

You've got this Jackson, just be yourself. Wait, umm. Well, fuck it!

Arriving at Howie's place, promptly at seven, I depressed the call button, and he buzzed me right up. As I climbed the stairs to his third-floor apartment, my senses were assaulted by delectable scents I hoped were coming from his place. Ascending the final steps, his smiling face awaited me in the hall as a sense of comfort washed through me.

"Always so prompt, just like at the coffee shop." He smiled, leaning against the doorframe.

"I pride myself on it. Here." I handed him the bag. "I didn't know which you preferred so I bought one of each."

Curious, he peeked inside. "Hmm, red and white. A man after my own heart, come in."

Noticing his shoes sitting just inside the doorway, I toed mine off as I took the time to glance around. While his place was small, it was tidy with original hardwood floors throughout. On the far wall there was a door at each end, between it sat a queen-sized bed and single nightstand. He'd set up the center of the studio apartment space as a makeshift living room with a couch facing a TV that sat atop a stand and an old trunk serving as a coffee table. To the left of that was the small galley kitchen where he was currently working.

"Anything I can help with?" I asked as I watched him stir the sauce that was the heavenly scent that had filled the stairwell.

"I'm good, thanks for asking. Why don't you pick a wine and pour us each a glass? Opener is in the drawer in front of you, and the glasses are above your head."

I grabbed what was needed and proceeded to pour. "It smells wonderful, what are we having?" I inquired, setting a glass beside his workstation.

"Eggplant parmesan," he informed me, spooning some sauce. "Here, tell me if it's missing anything."

It tasted even better than it smelled, my eyes rolled back, and I couldn't help the moan that escaped. Cooking was not my forte, I basically lived on takeout so having a home cooked meal was more than appreciated by me. "This is wonderful."

"Thank you," he said and bowed. "I wasn't sure if you were a vegetarian or not, so I erred on the side of caution."

"Nope, I'm a carnivore who loves veggies." I winked. "What else can I help with?"

"The table is already set. Let me put this in the oven, dinner will be ready in about twenty minutes so let's enjoy our wine on the couch while we wait."

So far, so good. Conversation wasn't my strong suit, but it was too late to abort the mission now.

"Breathe Jackson, I don't bite. Unless you want me to that is?" He flirted.

His brazen words aroused me. Swallowing hard, I could feel my Adam's apple bob as I tracked those glorious lips gripping the edge of his wine glass. Tilting it, the red liquid slid between them. The same lips I've dreamed about for months, wrapped around my cock as I uttered words of praise in return. He must've seen the look in my eyes, or the bulge in my pants as the look he gave me in return was beyond heated.

The air crackled around us as he took the glass from my hand, setting it down. Cemented in place, I could only watch as Howie slid across, straddling my lap.

"Is this okay?" he asked. Nodding in response I assured him I was more than okay with it. He pulled my shirt aside, just enough so his lips could graze the collarbone beneath it. Kissing his way up, he stopped at my ear whispering, "Is this still okay?"

Breathlessly I panted, "Yes."

Across my cheekbone his lips trailed, leaving tingles in their wake until finally descending upon mine. Tentatively he kissed me, my hands slid around his waist. When his tongue traced the slit between them, my lips parted and he slid his tongue in, catching mine. A clashing of tongue and teeth ensued, clumsy as it may've been it by far exceeded any encounter I'd had to date. The feeling of finally having Howie within reach fulfilled needs I'd long since repressed.

Firmly gripping his hips, I glided him back and forth against my straining erection. God, how long had it been since I'd had a release not by my own hand? Breaking for air, I panted, "Howie," almost pleadingly, begging for more.

"Fucking hell, this is beyond intense," he groaned just as the oven timer dinged.

CHAPTER FIVE

Howie

I must say, that was a first for me, but then again this was also the first time I'd cooked for a man that wasn't merely a friend. Snagging a quick peck, I reluctantly slid from his lap to finish our dinner preparations. After all, I did promise the man a meal and had spent the last two hours preparing it.

Without a word, I removed the casserole dish from the oven and began retrieving the salad and bread. All the while my thoughts never veered from what had just happened. I'd promised myself I wouldn't move too fast yet there I was, straddling his lap like a jockey riding a prized stallion. Given my track record, he'd be gone after getting his fill and I didn't want that, not with Jackson. With him, I wanted so much more.

"Howie," he said, turning me to face him. "Talk to me."

"I don't want this to be over," I mumbled, barely above the music I had streaming.

"We haven't had dinner yet. Did I do something wrong?" His mournful glance matched the pain I felt inside.

"No one ever comes back after they get what they want. I don't want that to happen with you," I said sharing my worst fear.

"Oh Howie..." He began, cupping my face with his hands. "You have no idea how long it took me to work up the courage to even ask you out. A one and done isn't an option for me, not with you." Jackson leaned down, placing his forehead to mine. "You're worth so much more than that."

I wanted his words to be the truth. God how I wanted to believe what he was saying but I'd been here before. Told all the right things before the condom hit the trash can and their feet pounded against the pavement. Leaving me lost and, once again, alone.

"Here, let me help." He grabbed the salad and breadbasket while I carried the casserole dish to the table. We filled our plates in tandem silence, his pleasurable groan was the first sound to break the ice as he enjoyed his first bite. "This is fantastic. Where'd you learn how to cook?"

"I have a major addiction to all things Giada De Laurentiis. I own every one of her cookbooks. Met her once at a signing at the bookstore next to Northgate." My giddiness returned at the mention of my favorite Food Network chef.

"Remind me to thank her if our paths ever cross," he said, taking another bite.

The conversation flowed once more, but I couldn't ignore the voices in my head reminding me I wasn't worth more than a one-night stand. That I was so far out of Jackson's league that I was wasting our time by trying to impress him.

With dinner behind us and the kitchen cleaned, we returned to the couch but instead of sitting next to him I chose to sit at the far end.

"Come here," he patted the cushion beside him. Hesitantly I moved, as he wrapped his arm around me. "Howie, thank you for dinner. It was wonderful."

Here we go, the final kiss off. But...

"I'd like to see you again."

What? Wait for it, wait for it.

"Have you been to Leavenworth?" he asked, rubbing his hand up and down my spine. My head laid against his chest as I listened to his beating heart.

"The prison?"

He laughed. "No, the town in Washington. It's modeled after a Bavarian village. It's a two-hour drive from here. We could do a day trip, stroll through town and have lunch before heading home. Does that sound like something you'd enjoy?"

My inner child was doing summersaults and cartwheels. Was this guy for real? No one had ever taken me out on an actual date let alone to an out of town excursion. "I'd really like that, Jackson."

We made plans for the following Sunday, leaving bright and early before I walked him to the door, and we sealed the perfect evening with a kiss as we stood under the threshold to my home. This night of firsts had me rethinking the conclusions I'd instantly drawn and now regretted. *Maybe things would be okay after all.*

Jackson came into the café every day that week, on time like always, but instead of mumbling his order and walking away, he greeted me each morning with a smile and a kiss. We'd flirt across the room, talking as time would allow but never once did he pretend like he didn't know me. So many guys I'd slept with would walk right by me on the street, never acknowledging my presence as though I wore a cloak of invisibility. Jackson, he was different and every day I spent with him I felt the dark cloud shrouding my heart, really my life being cast away.

On Sunday, he once again greeted me with his customary good morning kiss, a latte, and a raspberry muffin at eight a.m. sharp. We chatted during the drive to Leavenworth about the one hit wonders of the eighties we both loved and were currently listening to. Funny thing was, neither of us enjoyed them in their heyday yet we were still drawn to their whimsical lyrics and uplifting beats.

When we pulled into Leavenworth, the quaint town instantly captured my heart. Strolling down its narrow lanes, I was transported back in time. I'd lost track of the number of candy stores we visited as I had more than my fair share of taffy. Jackson was currently dining on a Bavarian pretzel that was the size of his head, his youthful exuberance filled me with hope. We sat in the park at the center of town, listening to the polka band play and basking in the afternoon sun. Jackson bought me a refrigerator magnet to commemorate our day date before taking me to dinner at the local German restaurant. Once we'd eaten our fill of *rouladden* and *spaetzle*, we headed back to Seattle, but I didn't want this day to end.

CHAPTER SIX

Jackson

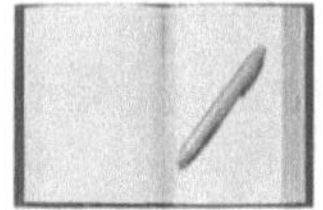

I wasn't ready for our date to be over, but I didn't want Howie to think that this was the *'over and I was done with him'* scenario he feared. I wanted more, I'd waited far too long to ask him out and I longed to be a more permanent fixture in his life. *Would he think my question was too much too soon?*

The silence in the car was unbearable and that wasn't how I wanted things to be between us.

"Talk to me Howie, tell me what you're thinking," I asked, taking his hand. As I glanced across the front seat at him, he lifted his gaze from his lap and met mine.

"I'm just having a hard time believing this is real?" he admitted.

"Howie, I don't want to scare you away but … I'm not really sure what the words are that I'm looking for. I guess what I'm asking is, will you be my boyfriend? Is that how this still works? I'm so, ugh…" I felt like a fool having asked that, but it'd been so long since I was in a relationship that I didn't even know if we called each other boyfriends. Significant others? Exclusive? The terminology was lost on me, and this wasn't a fictional story where my written words could call it whatever I deemed it to be. This was real life, which unfortunately was something I was nowhere near being in tune with.

"You want to be my boyfriend?" He turned those hazel puppy dog eyes my way, brimmed with unshed tears.

"I'm sorry, I didn't mean to make you cry. Shit, I screwed that up, didn't I?" Great, now my ignorance went and fucked up the only good thing I had in my life right now. Howie.

"No one ever thought I was boyfriend material before," he spoke into his lap, fiddling with the zipper on his jacket. *Oh…*

"Their loss is hopefully my gain. So will you cut an old, out of the loop man a break on his inability to keep up with modern-day terminology and say you'll be mine?" I hope the sincerity in my statement was felt how I meant it to come across.

"Oh Jackson." He smiled, and the first tear broke free leaving a gleaming trail in its wake. "I've been yours since the first day you walked into the café. I'd love to be exclusive and FYI, you know you're only eight years older than me, so you are nowhere near the old man category."

The playful banter I'd grown to love over the many nights we'd recently spent talking on the phone slid back into place after that. My inept question seemed to be what Howie needed to tamper the inner turmoil he had brewing. To say he'd spent his life surrounded by idiots who'd missed everything that made him the wonderful man he was would be putting it mildly. The fact that I saw all the great things that encompassed his being made me feel better about myself, and I couldn't wait to show Howie the exact opposite of everything he'd been wrongly led to believe he was.

"Hey," Howie said as I pulled up in front of his building. "Why don't you park and come up for some coffee?"

Saying no wasn't an option as I wasn't ready to say goodnight to my new beau. I longed to learn all things

Howie. What made him tick, his likes and dislikes. His wishes and dreams, something inside of me was yearning to be the one to make them come true. With that last shocking realization fresh in my mind, I followed his directions around to the side of the building where the parking garage was located and claimed one of the guest spots.

We walked hand in hand up the narrow staircase, my eyes never veering from the beautiful attribute poised in front of me. Brazenly, I leaned forward, nipping a cheek through his jeans and eliciting the most delightful squeal from the man who was burrowing himself deeper inside the vault I'd kept locked inside for far too long. Or maybe not; maybe Howie was the only one who had the combination to it and he was the one I'd been waiting patiently for.

Down, Jackson, don't scare him away.

I'd always been one to wear my thoughts and feelings on my sleeve for others to see. My mother was the one who'd always told me to be true to myself, not let others guide me and enjoy all that life had to offer. Not a day passed that I didn't miss her. Her smile, the way she could turn every negative into a positive. She was a beautiful woman with a deep soul and a heart of gold.

Silently, we toed off our shoes just inside the door before he asked, "Would you like some coffee? Tea?" He paused, waiting for my response.

"I'd like to have you if I could, please?"

CHAPTER SEVEN

Howie

I couldn't move, couldn't muster a single thought let alone utter one word. Had he heard me say those exact words to Lexi?

"Too much, too fast?" he questioned. "Sorry, I didn't mean to scare you. I'll just, um, I'll just go." I watched as he walked to the door in stunned silence. *He's walking away Howie, stop him!*

"Stop!" I yelled, and he flinched. "Sorry, I didn't mean to yell. Please don't go."

"Really?"

"Really. Did you, did you hear me say that to Lexi?" I had to know.

"Tell Lexi what?" he questioned.

"Coffee, tea, or me?" I stated, well more like questioned. Could this truly have been a coincidence?

"I'm sorry, I'm not following." He stood against the back of the couch, waiting for me to explain.

How can this be?

"Never mind, do you want something to drink?" I needed to get out of this conversation having already made a complete fool of myself.

"Howie, you're flustered, and I'm confused. Come here," he said, opening his arms and I knew I couldn't refuse. As soon as my head hit his chest he wrapped them around me. "Okay, now explain the beverage reference."

"Ugh, do I have to?" I half-ass begged, knowing he wasn't gonna let it go.

"Yes, please?" he asked, stroking my back and kissing the top of my head. Little did he know, he already had me. I was a goner for Jackson, hook, line, and sinker.

"Just to clarify," I began with my face still buried against his chest. "You never overheard me saying any part of that to Lexi?"

"Nope, it's virginal to my ears." He laughed. "Now spill."

"Okay, okay. So, on one of the mornings you came in and ignored my advances for like the millionth time I mumbled to myself, well I'd hoped to myself, but it turns out that Lexi was standing close enough to hear," I paused, so not ready to blurt out the embarrassing part.

"For the record," Jackson said. "I wasn't ignoring your advances. I was ignoring my desire for you."

Well now, that's a whole different ball game.

I glanced up, meeting his gaze. "You wanted me?"

His lips found mine and he murmured, "More than you know. Now quit procrastinating and finish." He smiled and kissed me again. Giving me the courage I needed without knowing it to continue.

"The poet in me escaped and I mumbled, every day he comes in and orders coffee or tea. Oh, how I wish he'd order me." Fucking hell, my face heated up to an uncontrollable level, so I buried it in his armpit.

"Howie..." He chuckled. "As much as I love having you in my arms, that can't be an ideal spot to put your face."

Oddly enough, all I could smell was his deodorant. Musky, with a light floral hint. Two scents I'd now forever associate with Jackson. *Wait, did he just say he loved having me in his arms? Oh shit, did I sniff too loudly? Great, now he's gonna think I have an armpit fetish. Ugh...*

"Hey, my little poet," he said, lifting my chin. "You're fucking adorable."

"Glad you think so 'cause I feel like a total dumbass right now," I whined, wishing I could evaporate into the hardwoods beneath us.

Jackson paused, his lips within reach of mine. "I do think so. Now that I know my words didn't offend you, I'd like to get back to enjoying our evening." He slid over the back of the couch, taking me with him. Laughter filled the air before it was silenced as our mouths met once again.

Things heated up between us as desire raged through me. I'd never had another man kiss me so fervently, passionately, his actions making promises without spoken words. This was our second official date, the most anyone ever saw me was twice but he was the first one who'd ever expressed interest in dating me. Making me a *real* boyfriend as opposed to someone they only fucked. My hormones were begging for me to strip us both naked and get to it, but my heart wrestled with that idea fearing the end would come if I offered myself to Jackson.

"Hey," he said as he pulled back. "You still here with me?" I nodded, but he wasn't buying it. "Howie, we have all the time in the world. Don't rush what you're not ready to do. I'm happy just spending time with you."

And trigger the waterworks...

"Howie, baby what's wrong?" He sat up, drawing me onto his lap. "Talk to me."

"Boyfriends? Being with me? Baby? Where did you come from?" I questioned, wiping my face with my shirt.

"Sorry, was the pet name too much?"

"Too much?" I laughed, rather maniacally. "Why are you being so nice to me?"

"Because I like you, Howie. I hate that others have made you think so little of yourself. You're fun to be around, you treat people with respect, even when they don't deserve it. I watch you work, everything you do is with purpose and a need to please. Customers return to see you, and they greet you like a long-lost friend and you do the same in return. The quiet, introverted girl who comes in and orders the same thing every Friday morning. You call her by her name and her face lights up. Someone paid attention to her and that makes her day, gives her a reason to push on. You remember her order, ask how she's doing, and you pay attention to her answer. You may think your job is simple, purposeless, but from my side of the counter I see how much of a difference you make to everyone who comes into the café."

Now I'd been reduced to big ass baby status for a whole other reason. I'm not nice to people because I have to be, I'm nice to people because I want to be. It makes me feel good when I help others, fills me with pride. I may not have much to offer, but what I do have in abundance is kindness. That's a gift that's easy and free to give.

"Howie…" He took my face in his hands, a gesture that warmed me each time. "You're beautiful, inside and out." His lips kissed away the dampness the tear streaks left behind before finding their place against mine. Our tongues were sliding in and out in their own dance. The erection that had long since waned, rejoined the celebration. Jackson unzipped my pants, his fingertip trailed teasingly along my briefs outlining my cock before his hand slid inside the cotton confines and he gripped it firmly.

I hissed, loving the feel of his hand on my hardened skin but fought the urge to fuck myself into oblivion in his tight grasp.

"Baby." He nipped my collar bone. "Let me take care of you tonight."

"Mmm, hmm," I muttered, lost in the moment.

Jackson guided me up on my knees, pulling my pants down enough to free my erection. Giving it a couple rough tugs, his words surprised me as he uttered, "Fuck my mouth."

"Huh?" The heat in his eyes bore through to my soul as I still was unable to comprehend his words.

He licked a stripe up the shaft. "Fuck, my, mouth." He drew the tip inside and I shuddered. Having never been told to do this by another, made this a completely foreign concept I was unable to wrap my brain around. Jackson grabbed hold of my ass, propelling me forward and deeper into the confines of his mouth.

"Fuck," I muttered. I had to brace my palms on the back of the couch to keep from collapsing. His demanding hands guided me in and out, humming around my overly sensitive cock. It wouldn't take long before I'd blow, not only had it been for-*fucking*-ever since I'd been laid, but never *ever* had another made sure I was so thoroughly cared for. If I opened my eyes and saw my dick sliding in and out of those gorgeous lips I'd been sucking on mere moments ago, that would surely take me over the edge.

Even with my eyes tightly closed, the end was nearing as his oral talents far surpassed his literary works in this moment. This man's mouth and tongue had talents of their own. As he swirled his tongue around the head, his fingertip teased my entrance and that was all it took for my release to surge forward. In this clouded state of mind, I'd forgotten to warn the gorgeous man below me as I unloaded months' worth of reserves into his willing orifice.

CHAPTER EIGHT

Jackson

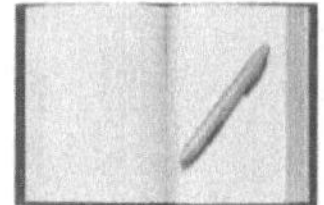

Howie was reduced to putty after he came. Limply, he slid onto the couch beside me with his eyes shut, completely blissed out. The surprised look on his face when I directed him to fuck my mouth told me no one had ever said those words to him before. I just wanted to wrap him up in a cocoon and do all I could to make sure no one ever hurt him again. When he told me the limerick he'd recited about coffee and tea, I knew I was a goner. He'd wanted me for as long as I'd wanted him.

"Howie?" I nudged him. "Are you alright?"

"Oh my God, oh my God. I'm so sorry, you probably need me to take care of you now." He hopped up and reached for my pants, but I gently grabbed his hands, entwining our fingers.

"Hey, I didn't do this expecting anything in return." He turned his deer in the headlights stare on me. "This was something I wanted to do for you."

"Wha— what?" he stuttered, something I was growing accustomed to. I didn't like it as each time it reminded me how poorly others had treated him.

"Come on, let me tuck you in before I head out." I stood, walking him backward. I had him stripped down to his boxers by the time we reached the bed. Silently, he climbed in as I took a seat on the bed beside him. "Next Saturday night, how about dinner at my place at seven?"

"I'd like that." He grinned so wide I knew I'd done the right thing and hopefully proved to him that I was here for more than just a fuck. I wanted the whole deal with Howie, and I'd do everything in my power to continue proving that to him.

I leaned over and kissed his forehead before reaching his mouth. "Sweet dreams Howie."

His heavily lidded eyes barely opened. "Yes, I'm sure they will be," he sleepily uttered.

The ridiculous smirk I wore home couldn't have been erased if I'd tried. We'd reached our first hurdle as a couple, and rode across it together. While communication hadn't always been my strong suit, I'd make sure it would now be in order to keep the man who was quickly taking owner-ship of my heart.

The erection from earlier hadn't waned, and neither had the memories I'd just made with Howie. As soon as I got home, I climbed in the shower, lathered up, reached down and after several calculated strokes I came harder than I had in a long time. It didn't take much to reach the climax I sought as I pictured Howie's handsome face as he came in my mouth earlier when I'd pleasured him. That look of pure ecstasy would be my undoing. Thoughts of the many things I'd love to do to that body of his filled my dreams as well as the notebook I kept on the bedside table. When the idea for a new story came to mind, I grabbed it and began filling its empty pages. Writers were never far from their tools, nor from their next musing.

Romance wasn't a genre I'd ever delved into, the major-ity of what I wrote was either sci-fi or murder mystery, but Howie shed a new light on it for me. Romance, well that wasn't for me but erotic romance now that I could wrap my proverbial pen around. The pep in my step on Monday as I entered the café had his name written all over it. I stood in line as I did every weekday morning for not only my culinary treat, but the good morning kiss my boyfriend had waiting for me.

"Good morning, my muse," I said, leaning over the counter and taking the offering he had.

"Good morning to you, too. To what do I owe the new term of endearment to?" he grinned. That face, this man, was the one I'd been longing for. The one to draw me from my shell and make me whole again.

"Do you read?" I asked as he scanned my card, although I now noticed I was receiving the customary ten percent employee discount he was allotted with each purchase.

He winked. "I've read a few tales by the famous Jackson Milsap."

The surprised response I returned exited as a gasp. "You read my books?"

"Not all, yet, so far only two but everything you've written has been purchased and is queued up in my Kindle app," he proudly boasted as he handed me the receipt.

"Well," I paused, tucking my wallet away. "I hope you'll enjoy the new one I'm starting today, inspired by a hot barista working in a local coffee shop." I blew him a kiss as I walked to my usual table, feeling his stare on my backside the whole way.

As soon as my computer booted up, I opened a new doc and the story poured effortlessly from me. I became lost in a new world with Howie fresh on my mind. I'd never had words flow so freely as they were right now. Time was of no essence as I'd chosen to self-publish this book when it was done, but I hadn't realized lunch had long since passed until Howie placed a sandwich and chips in front of me.

"Thank you, love," I said without thinking, but Howie's bright smile beaming back reassured me that my faux pas wasn't ill received.

I should be nervous with how quickly things were falling into place between us, but I wasn't. It felt like I'd been waiting forever to find him. That compounded with how long it took my dumbass to finally ask him out, had me leaving matters in fate's hands. All that really mattered was that this worked for us as a team, but as usual my overly compulsive devil's advocate side weaseled its way in whenever I let my guard down the slightest bit. That would be a battle I'd forever be locked in and would take some time for me to learn to ignore.

"Like what you see?" Howie asked, drawing me from the trance my wandering mind had me in.

"More than you know," I unabashedly admitted.

My words must've struck a chord as he leaned over, claiming my lips in a possessive kiss that had my toes curling. Seeing Howie every day made it more bearable to wait until the weekends for our dates. In essence, each day I spent here was a day date for us. We had breakfast and lunch in the same general vicinity, sneaking kisses and touches here and there. Some nights Howie had to close and I needed to write, so we talked on the phone until we could no longer hold our eyes open. If my focus were more on my work and less on Howie, I'd get more done during the day. As it was, I was having to spend the evenings alone in my writing cave in order to meet the deadlines I had.

By the end of the day, I had the first ten thousand words of the manuscript typed up and couldn't have been happier with my progress. That was by far one of the most productive days I'd had in a long time, and I owed it all to Howie. I stayed until the coffee shop closed at five, then walked my man home before continuing onto my place to start developing a marketing strategy for the new literary road I was embarking upon. New sites to promote it on, an editor, and cover designer. The list was endless, but I was excited to do the research.

Come Wednesday, I'd reached the point of the story where a major turning point would need to take place in order to keep the reader engaged. Up until now, things had been progressing much as Howie and I had been in real life, but it needed something more. It was a difficult mindset to get myself into. The idea of losing Howie or having something happen to him was unbearable to think about. I'd never directly written a character mirroring a real person, only those loosely based on others. *Maybe this book wasn't such a good idea after all.*

"Ugh," I groaned, burying my face in my hands.

"What's wrong handsome?" Howie asked, pulling my hands away and plopping down on my lap. My hands instinctively wound around him.

"I'm at a crucial turning point in the book and I'm having a hard time figuring it out. I'm too close to the characters and its messing with my head." I chose to keep my response somewhat elusive as to not give too much away. I guess I should've run it past him first to make sure it was all right to write a book modeled after us.

"What do you mean?" he asked, tucking a piece of hair behind my ear, reminding me I was overdue for a cut.

"Well, I um..." As I took a moment to choose my words wisely, the bell over the door chimed and in walked a handful of customers.

"Duty calls." He kissed me before flitting away.

I dwelled on the dilemma I'd created for myself for the remainder of the afternoon. While I didn't want to think about bad things happening to Howie, the only way I'd be able to properly portray the feelings I needed to convey to the readers would be to allow those thoughts into my head so I could get into character.

CHAPTER NINE

Howie

Since Wednesday afternoon, Jackson had been keeping to himself. He still came into the café every day, greeted me with a kiss and walked me home after my shift, but the light that had been in his eyes was gone. *Had I overstepped when I planted myself on his lap? PDA hadn't seemed to be a problem for him but maybe that was too much? Or else, he'd had his fill of me already. Well, at least this one left before he fucked me ... but he'd be taking a piece of my heart with him.*

On Saturday, I wasn't sure what was going on because nothing else had been said about our date. Rather than waiting for him, I felt I needed to get the inevitable let-down I felt was coming out of the way.

Hey, I texted him.

Hey yourself.

Are we still on for tonight or do you need to cancel?

Cancel???

Yeah, you haven't said much these last two days, so I wasn't sure if our date was still on. My thumb paused, hovering over the send button as I toyed with whether or not to delete my comment. But really, what did I have to lose at this point if he was already of the mindset that this was over between us?

Oh, sorry. Yes, we're still on, we need to talk. Jackson sent back.

Here it comes, "we need to talk" never bodes well for the one on the receiving end of whatever is about to be dished out.

In my frantic state of mind, I cleaned. I always disinfected my place from top to bottom when my anxiety was working overtime. I ripped the linens off the bed, washed them, steamed the wood floors, scrubbed the bathroom tile floor by hand, sanitized the toilet, sink and shower, and even wiped the windows until they sparkled.

I was a hot mess by the time I arrived at Jackson's. I'd not bothered to bring wine or anything for that matter but maybe I should've. Timidly, I forced myself to depress the intercom button and announce my arrival for which he immediately buzzed me up. Every step I took up the narrow staircase felt like I was walking the plank. I'd grown so accustomed to Jackson and the natural way things fell into place for us. I guess that's what I get for thinking I deserved to be happy. When I reached his door, it was propped open so I stepped inside as quietly as I could but didn't take off my shoes as I assumed I wouldn't be staying long. Taking the time to put them on while trying to bolt before the tears fell wasn't something I wanted to contend with.

The door squeaked as I shut it, alerting him that I was there. "I hope you like spaghetti. I'm not the best cook, but I can read a recipe," he said before turning around. "Howie, what's wrong?" Jackson put the lid on the pot before embracing me. As soon as I was in his arms, the waterworks I'd been trying my best to stave came rushing forth. "Oh baby, what happened?"

"You— you— you—" I stuttered, sounding like a complete fool. "Wanted to talk."

"Yeah, and—?"

"You're breaking up with me!" I half yelled, bawling like a baby.

"I am?" he questioned, completely confused by my outburst.

"Isn't that what you wanted to tell me?"

"No, it's quite the opposite actually. Come on, let's sit down," he said as he led us over to the couch but kept his arm around me the entire way. Once seated, he pulled me onto his lap, this seems to be the customary position to have me in whenever we talked. "Oh Howie, I'm so sorry. You'd think as a writer I'd have better control over the way I worded things. I just got you, there's no way in hell I'm letting you go."

"Really?" I questioned skeptically.

"Really, really baby," he cupped my face, brushing away the tears with the pads of his thumbs, "I love you."

"Oh my God Jackson, I'm so in love with you." For the first time in my life, I was crying happy tears. Not only did someone finally want me, but it was the someone I wanted most in return. Although I still had no idea what he wanted to talk about, when his lips met mine, and his tongue swept the inside of my mouth I... *ohh squirrel!*

Jackson was the one to break the kiss first, I was struck with the inability to muster a complete thought between his declaration and the searing kiss that followed.

"Howie, I want to talk to you about my book. I'm not breaking up with you."

"Ugh, you went silent after I jumped in your lap, and I thought maybe I'd gone too far with the PDA and you were pulling away from me."

"Ha-ha, no. You did surprise me when you hopped on, but it was a good surprise. I just need you to be Howie, don't do anything you're not comfortable with. If you feel the need to jump on my lap, then do so although I don't recommend it if I'm meeting with my publisher," Jackson joked.

"Okay, I'm sorry I overreacted, but you've been really weird since then." Something was up and before I could set my insecurities to rest, I really needed to find out what it was.

"I'm sorry I didn't clarify my comment. I totally understand why you assumed the worst and I promise to work on communicating better. Now, back to business. As you know, I've been working on the barista story." I smiled, remembering him telling me this and calling me his muse. "Well, I reached an impasse I was having a challenge overcoming."

"About the dramatic turning point?" I asked.

"Yes, exactly. When I write, I need to get into my characters' heads which, in this case, is both of us. I had to come up with something I didn't want to think about in order to make the scene work. I'll be honest, it scared and depressed the fuck out of me. The thought of anything happening to you sent a flood of emotions through me that I wasn't prepared to dissect. When I did, it dawned on me that the reason I was struggling was because I'm in love with you and I'd do anything and everything in my power to protect you. I also realized that I hadn't asked for your permission to include our relationship in this story which was what we needed to talk about." His eyes searched mine, seeking my approval or denial.

"I think having my boyfriend write a story that I inspired is, well, super freaking cool for lack of a more mature response. Can I just ask one thing of you though?" I chewed on my bottom lip, waiting for him to reply.

"Of course."

"Please don't kill me off. Other than that, I'm honored to be a part of it." His full-bodied laugh surprised me but lightened the intensity of our conversation which we desperately needed. How could he ever think I'd be mad that he was writing a fictional story based upon us? To me, that was the highest honor I'd ever received, and I was now itching to read it.

"Howie, to kill you off would be to kill a part of me. There's not a snowball's chance in hell I'm doing that, my love."

I'm someone's love, somebody finally loves me.

CHAPTER TEN

Jackson

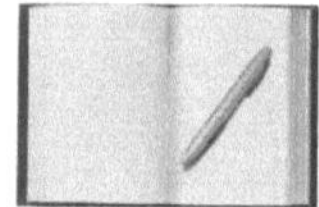

I can't believe the hell I'd put my poor guy through. I'm gifted with wordsmithing, even have the awards to prove it, yet made such a rookie mistake in texting. No wonder so many chide the use of technology as a form of communication, so much can be perceived from written, or in our case unwritten, words and obscure texts.

"Come on." I smacked his ass and he squealed. "Let's eat."

"I'm starving."

"You pour the wine and I'll get the food. The wine is in the fridge. If you hate it, blame it on the food channel." I directed him as I filled our plates, meeting at the table I'd already set. The mournful look he had we he arrived had long since faded, for that I was beyond thankful. I'd be beating myself up over this until the day I die.

"My God, this is fantastic," he said, slurping a string of spaghetti. The infamous scene from *Lady and the Tramp* crossed my mind.

"Howie..." I reached across the table, taking his hand in mine. "Say you'll stay the night with me?" Why was I so nervous asking that? I'd been biding my time, wanting to prove to him that I was in this for the long haul before we finally made love. I wanted everything to be right for him. He was more than worth the wait, but the need to be with him as one was important to me as well. This was the major turning point in our life, and I didn't want to mess it up.

He smiled. "I'd like that."

We cleaned up the kitchen as a team and once the dishwasher was going, we curled up on the couch and selected a movie to watch on Netflix. Midway through, Howie was softly snoring beside me, so I shut it off and carried him to bed before jumping in the shower. As soon as I stepped under the spray, a pair of arms snaked around my waist.

"I thought you were sleeping?" I asked but was more than happy to share a shower with him.

"I woke up in time to see your naked ass streak across the room."

I peeked over my shoulder, eyeing him. "Streak huh?"

"It was better than watching the movie." He reached around, sliding his hand around my cock. "I've been waiting for this," he said, giving it a couple strokes.

"Me too, love." I could feel his erection grinding against my ass. Turning, our hardened members met at the same time as our lips did. Feeling his flesh against mine heightened the urgency I had to be buried inside him. We took turns under the spray, our hands exploring unchartered flesh as this was the first time we'd been fully naked in front of each other. We did our best to wash, albeit haphazardly, before shutting off the water. Wrapping a towel around him, I pulled him against me. We became a tangled mess of lips and limbs, barely drying ourselves off before tumbling down on the bed.

I'd been dreaming of this moment for weeks. Seeing this side of Howie showcased him in a new light to me. Messy wet hair, kiss swollen lips, his cock warming the palm of my hand as I stroked him. But I needed more, I needed to taste every inch of this gorgeous man I was sharing my bed with for hopefully a lot longer than just one night.

I slinked down the bed, leaving a trail of kisses down his torso before swirling my tongue around the tip of his cock and working my way down his shaft. Taking each ball in turn, I gently licked and sucked as his soft moans filled the air and I longed to hear more from him. Nudging his legs apart, I positioned myself between them, lifting his hips as my tongue teased his opening. His moans deepened and the sounds he emitted had my cock throbbing with need. When I had his outer ring nice and wet, I spread his cheeks and dove in. His groans quickly turned to incoherent murmurs as I slid a finger inside. Fingering a partner was one of my favorite things to do. A second finger joined the first, scissoring inside his tight channel, when I crooked them and grazed his spot, he arched up and I knew he was almost ready for me to enter him.

Reluctantly I removed the digits which was met with a low growl. "Don't worry baby, I'll make it up to you," I told him as I sheathed and lubed my cock before lining it up at his entrance. Taking his lips in mine, I pushed in easily past the first ring but paused once there so he could adjust to the intrusion. When he wrapped his legs around my waist and tried to ride me, I knew he was ready for more.

God, the tightness enveloping me was overwhelming. I needed to move, needed to release but wouldn't allow myself to do so until Howie came first. This wasn't about me or him getting off; this was about tightening the bond we were forming and being a selfish lover would never enter into our love making.

"Jackson," he whispered, laced with need.

"I know, baby, I feel it too." I pulled out, sliding back in with a single thrust, repeating the motion until I found a grove that pegged his spot.

"There," he moaned, and I increased the motions. Sweat beaded my forehead as the climax built at the base of my spine intensified almost painfully. "Oh, God, Jackson," he said, tightly fisting my hair. The slight pain only furthered my arousal as I pounded harder, awaiting the words I so desperately needed to hear. "I'm coming."

His channel throbbed around me as he came. The elated sound that escaped his lips combined with his warm release spreading between us sent me over the edge.

"Howie," I panted as I pushed in as far as I could and came inside the man I loved, filling me with a sense of ease, a feeling of ... forever.

About TL Travis

TL Travis is an award-winning published author of LGBTQIA+ contemporary and paranormal romance and erotic musings that have earned "Best-Selling Author" flags in the US as well as Internationally.

In her free time, TL enjoys catching up with her family, attending concerts, wine tasting, and traveling.

TL is surrounded by her extensive 4-legged rescue pets, her sons, and adorable grandkids. She will continue saving furry friends in need for as long as she lives. Tl would like to remind you to "Adopt, not shop." Saving that lost soul may be just what you need.

Other Books By TL Travis

The Social Sinners Series:

Boxset:

https://books2read.com/SSWorldTour

Behind the Lights, 1

MM Coming of Age Rockstar Romance

In the Shadows, 2

MM Rockstar Hurt/Comfort Romance

A Heart Divided, 3

MMM Rockstar Romance

Beyond the Curtain, 4

MM BDSM Hurt/Comfort PTSD Rockstar Romance

After the Final Curtain, 5

MM BDSM Rockstar Romance

Maiden Voyage Series:

Boxset

Ryder's Guardian, 1

MM Rockstar Bodyguard Romance

Derek's Destiny, 2

MM Rockstar Teacher Romance

Jaxson's Nemesis, 3

MM Enemies to lovers Rockstar Romance

Shadow's Light, 4

MM Rockstar Hurt/Comfort Second Chance Romance

<u>Embrace The Fear (ETF) Series:</u>

Rhone's Rebel, 1

MM Hurt/Comfort Rockstar Romance

David's Disaster, 2

MM Daddy-boy Hurt/Comfort Rockstar Romance

Seltzer's Taylor, 3

11/3/2023

MM Rockstar Romance

His Final Chase, 4

MM Rockstar Daddy-Little Romance

11/2024

<u>Daddies and their Littles</u>

When Daddy Hurts

MM Daddy-Little Hurt/Comfort Romance

A Little Christmas: Jacob

MM Daddy-Little Hurt/Comfort Romance

A Little Christmas: Orion's Secret

MM Daddy-Little Hurt/Comfort Romance

<u>Pet Play</u>

Pick Us, Daddy

Pride Pet Play 2023 Series

https://books2read.com/PPP2023

<u>Standalone novels:</u>

Heat

MM Small Town Coming of Age Bear Bottom Romance

Only Time Will Tell

MM Coming of Age Time-Travel Romance

See Me

MM Hurt/Comfort Enemies to Lovers Body Posi-

tive/Disfigurement Romance

<u>Greyson Fox Saga (each can be read as a standalone):</u>

Greyson Fox

MM Erotic May/December Age-Gap First Time Coming

of Age Romance

Forgive Me Father

MM Coming of Age Hurt/Comfort Rent-a-boy Ro-

mance

<u>Stand-alone novelette's/novella's:</u>

Summer Boy

MM Small Town First-Time Coming of Age Demisexual Romance

Girl Crush

MF (1 scene)/ FF Sapphic Romance

What Works For Us

FF Over 40 Erotic Novelette

Rules of the Game

MM Erotic Workplace Romance

Coffee, Tea or Me?

MM Contemporary Romance

Penny For Your Thoughts

MM Contemporary Second Chance Holiday Romance

<u>**Paranormal Romance:**</u>

The Sebastian Chronicles

Historical Paranormal Erotic Romance

(Includes all 5 stories listed below)

Sebastian, The Beginning

MF Historical Paranormal Erotica

My Servant, My Lover

MF/MM Historical Paranormal Erotica

Wealthy Ménage

MF/MM/MFM/Ménage Historical Paranormal Erotica

Prohibition Inhibitions

MF/MM/MMF/MFM/BDSM Historical Paranormal Erotica

The Tryst - Chronicle Finale

MM Paranormal Erotic Romance

Pity the Living, Not the Dead

MM Paranormal First Time Dark Romance

MF Titles are published under Raven Kitts